The Night of the Hurricane's Fury

by **CANDICE RANSOM**

Illustrated by **PAUL TONG**

On My Own

HISTORY

M Millbrook Press/Minneapolis

for Alex
—C.R.

for Leigh, who makes all of my illustrations come to life
—P.T.

Millbrook Press
A division of Lerner Publishing Group, Inc.
241 First Avenue North
Minneapolis, MN 55401 U.S.A.

Website address: www.lernerbooks.com

Library of Congress Cataloging-in-Publication Data

Ransom, Candice F., 1952–
    The night of the hurricane's fury / by Candice Ransom ; illustrated by Paul Tong.
       p.   cm. — (On my own history)
    Summary: In 1900, while visiting his aunt in Galveston, Texas, ten-year-old Robert Pettibone is washed into swirling floodwaters when a hurricane takes the town by surprise.
    Includes bibliographical references (p.).
    ISBN 978–0–8225–7893–2 (lib. bdg. : alk. paper)
    1. Hurricanes–Texas–Galveston–Juvenile fiction. [1. Hurricanes–Texas–Galveston–Fiction. 2. Storms–Fiction. 3. Survival–Fiction. 4. Galveston (Tex.)–History–20th century–Fiction.] I. Tong, Paul, ill. II. Title.
    PZ7.R1743Ni 2009
    [Fic]–dc22   2008026491

Manufactured in the United States of America
1 2 3 4 5 6 – DP – 14 13 12 11 10 09

Author's Note

The summer of 1900 was a hot one in the United States. People tried to stay cool when temperatures topped 100 degrees. Everyone longed for rain and a breeze.

In the Atlantic Ocean, masses of moist, hot air and dry, chilly air bumped into each other, causing storms. Most of the storms lost energy over the wide, open waters and fizzled out.

A ship's captain noted a storm on August 27, 1900, but he didn't think it looked serious. Unlike the other squalls, this storm gained speed and force. It moved west, passing over Cuba and brushing Key West, Florida. When the storm hit the unusually warm waters of the Gulf of Mexico, it became stronger.

By the morning of Saturday, September 8, the storm headed for the Texas coast. In its path lay the city of Galveston, on Galveston Island. About 40,000 people lived in Galveston in 1900. The Jewel of Texas, as it was nicknamed, was a booming port and a popular vacation site. Sandy beaches and the warm climate made Galveston a pleasant place.

This is the story of what happened on the day everything changed for the people in Galveston. Ten-year-old Robert Pettibone was not a real person. But he could have been any of the boys who faced the fury of the deadliest hurricane to hit the United States.

Galveston Island, Texas
Saturday, September 8, 1900
Early Afternoon

Robert Pettibone slipped out
the front door and stood on the porch.
"Robert!" his aunt Maudie called
from the kitchen.
"Where are you going in this downpour?"
Robert didn't answer.
If he did, his aunt would make him
take an umbrella.
It was bad enough he always had
to wear a straw hat
and black wool stockings.
Robert saw two big boys
splashing down the street.
"I heard the waves are huge,"
one boy said to the other.

"Can I come too?"
Robert asked eagerly.
"Without your nanny?"
one boy jeered.
Laughing, the boys
headed toward the beach.

Earlier that summer, Robert had taken
a train from his home in Pennsylvania
to Galveston.
He had been sick all winter,
and his parents believed
the sea air would make him healthy.
So they sent him to stay with Aunt Maudie.
But Aunt Maudie wouldn't
let him go anywhere without her.
No wonder he didn't
have any friends in Galveston.

Robert jumped into the water
flowing down the street.
His boots got wet, but he didn't care.
He wanted to see the storm too!
Down at the beach, people gawked
at waves crashing
into the trolley-car track
that had been built out over the water.

The waters of the Gulf
were normally as still as a pond.
"Don't worry," a man told his wife.
"Our house is on stilts so
floodwaters will run underneath."
Like a giant's fist, a wave smacked the
bathhouses on the beach.
The shacks smashed into sticks.
Afraid, Robert turned to go back home.

At Aunt Maudie's, the water was up to

the bottom porch step.

Robert ran inside.

"Aunt Maudie!" he cried, breathless.

"The bathhouses are gone!"

Aunt Maudie swept into the hall,

carrying a wicker basket.

"I don't like the sound

of that wind," she said.

"I've packed clothes and food

and the family photographs.

We're going next door to the Russells'."

Outside, waves lapped the top porch step.

Rain stung their eyes

as they waded across the yard.

Boards, chairs, dishpans,
and other objects bobbed in the water.
"Look!" Robert exclaimed.
The boards were covered with
hundreds of tiny frogs.
It was as if the sky were raining frogs.
The Russells' house looked
like a floating island.
Robert half-swam, half-waded
to the porch.

Mr. Russell opened the front door.

The wind tore it out of his hands.

"Come in quick," he said.

Inside, at least 30 people

packed the parlor and dining room.

Aunt Maudie took the last seat.

Robert stood, wishing he had dry shoes.

Then he felt something cold
around his ankles.
Water slithered across the rug!
"Upstairs," said Mr. Russell.
"The water will never reach
the second floor."
Everyone hurried up the staircase.
Aunt Maudie steered Robert
into the bathroom.
Robert leaned against the wall.
The wind rammed the house
like a charging bull.
Robert felt the wall move.
"I think the house
is falling down!" he cried.
The wind lifted the roof,
then slammed it down again.
Robert looked out the window.

Something huge and dark
rushed toward them.
He glimpsed a mountain of water,
rooftops, buggies, furniture,
and trolley-car tracks.
Then he was knocked
into the bathtub.
The roof and walls
pulled apart like jaws, and
water gushed in.

The bathtub sailed through the gap,
and then floated in the surging flood.
Robert clung to the rim.
He heard the wails of
people thrown into the black water.
"Aunt Maudie!" he called.
But the wind tossed his
words away like rags.

Suddenly he felt a jarring bump.

The bathtub crashed into a house,

hurling Robert into the water.

He thrashed his legs, trying to swim.

But his heavy stockings and boots

dragged him down.

He kicked something hard.

A cart!

Robert hauled himself up on the cart.

He tugged off his boots and stockings.

Hot tears mingled with icy rain

on his cheeks.

Aunt Maudie was gone.

He was all alone.

Late Afternoon

Robert grasped the edge
of the cart with numb fingers.
The rain struck like needles.
The wind lashed at him.
Sometimes he heard cries for help.

Suddenly a flash of lightning
revealed an amazing sight.
Two men and three girls
were huddled on part of a house.
As Robert watched,
a big yellow dog scrambled
up onto the wreckage.
One of the men shouted with joy.
Was it his dog? Robert wondered.

"I'm here too!" Robert yelled.
But the water spun him
in another direction.
The next thing he knew,
a tree clobbered the cart.
Robert plunged into freezing water.
A branch stabbed his leg,
and warm blood streamed
from the wound.
Robert went under and then
surfaced again, sputtering.
His hands touched something
wet and soft.
It was the big dog!
Robert hooked one arm
around the dog's neck
and paddled with his feet.

At last, he and the dog
bumped into an upside-down table.
Robert climbed on top,
hauling the dog up beside him.
"I guess it's just you
and me," he said.

His leg was still bleeding.
He ripped his shirt and
wrapped it around his leg as a bandage.
The table thumped and banged
into underwater objects.
Robert held onto the dog
with one hand and
the table with the other.
He was still afraid, but
at least now he wasn't alone.

Evening

Thunk!
The table hit something
metal and solid.
Robert noticed rows of seats.
The metal thing was a trolley car.
Then he and the dog were
dunked underwater.
Gasping for breath,
Robert grabbed for the table.
If he let it get away,
they would die for sure.

Robert gripped the table's edge.
His fingernails dug into
soggy wood as he clawed up
the slanting top.
Inch by inch, he pulled himself
from the powerful current.
But where was the dog?
"Hello!" he called.

"Woof!" came an answering bark.

The dog thrust his head out of the water.

His teeth were bared in fear.

"Come on," Robert urged.

The dog flung his front paws
on the table.

The table tipped under his weight.

Robert began to slide off.

If he stayed on the table alone,

he would be okay.

But he would not let the dog drown.

"You rescued me," he said.

"Now it's my turn."

Reaching down, Robert lugged

the huge dog up beside him.

The table tipped dangerously.

Robert scooted over.

The table straightened again.
He would have to shift
his weight constantly
to keep the table from flipping over.
But for how long?
The storm had hammered
the city for hours.
How much longer would it last?
How much longer could he last?

Sunday, September 9
Dawn

Robert turned over.

Something warm and furry

moved under his arm.

He opened his eyes, remembering that

the table had struck

a tumbled-down house.

He and the dog had crawled

inside a second-story window.

Exhausted, they had fallen asleep.

Now Robert struggled across the slanted

floor to look out the window.

Pink light peeped from behind

broken clouds.

It was Sunday!

He had made it through the night!

But the soft pink glow

also showed a terrible sight.

The storm and flood had destroyed the city.

Buildings were gone.

Trees were uprooted.

In the middle of a pile of boards,

Robert saw a piano

like the one in Aunt Maudie's parlor.

The dog whimpered.

"You're hungry," Robert said.

"Me too."

He didn't know what to do or where to turn.

Then he heard a loud noise!

The bells of the Ursuline Convent rang out.

It was only a few blocks

from Aunt Maudie's house.

Nuns worshipped and studied there.

"We'll go to the convent,"

Robert told the dog.

"Maybe we'll see Aunt Maudie."

Carefully, they climbed
out the window and down
the mountain of rubble.
Only a few houses stood.
The rest had vanished or were blown over
like the one they had slept in.
"We'll follow the sound
of the bells," Robert said.

Slowly, they picked their way
through piles of boards, shingles,
glass, and puddles of water.
A horrible smell rose from the mess—muck
and rot and seaweed and dead animals.
In the mud, Robert saw
something else—human bodies.

Twisting his fingers
in the dog's yellow fur, he looked away.
"What will happen to us?"he asked.
"Will my folks ever find me?"

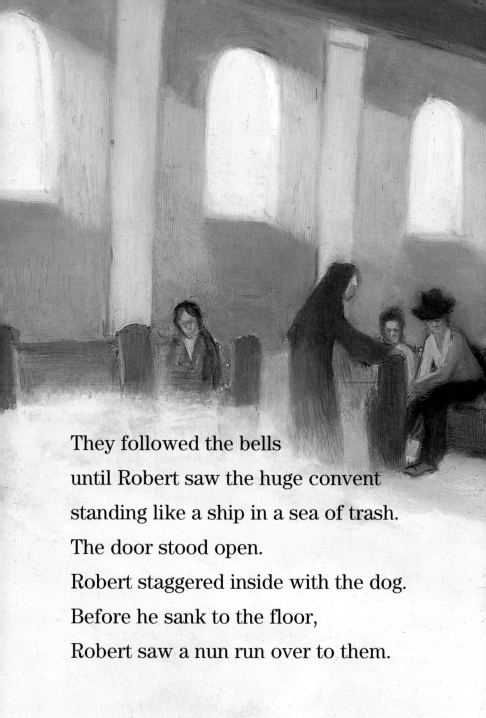

They followed the bells
until Robert saw the huge convent
standing like a ship in a sea of trash.
The door stood open.
Robert staggered inside with the dog.
Before he sank to the floor,
Robert saw a nun run over to them.

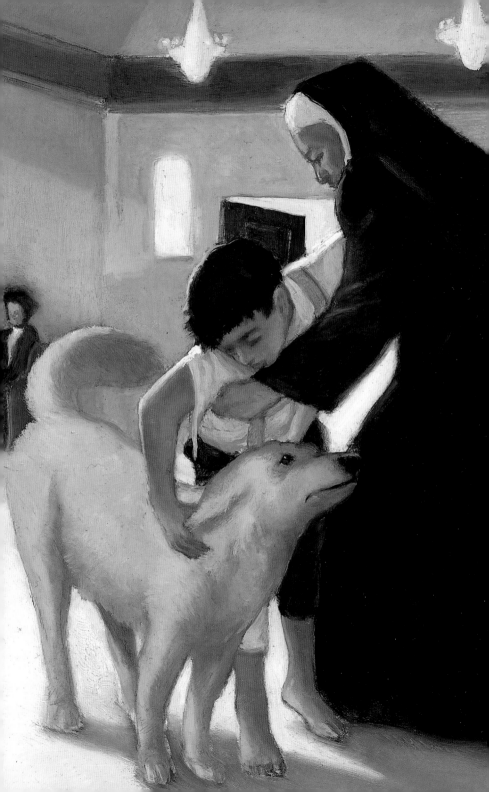

Saturday, September 15

Robert sat quietly,
looking out the train window.
His father dozed in the
seat across from him.
It had taken Robert's father
five days to travel from
Pennsylvania to Galveston.
Robert had stayed in the convent,
sleeping on the floor,
until his father had arrived.
He and his father had gone to hospitals,
looking for Aunt Maudie.
But they never found her.
"We must return to Pennsylvania,"
said Mr. Pettibone.

As the train clattered down the track,
Robert knew he was not the same boy
who had come to Galveston
earlier that summer.
He had survived the worst storm
the country had ever seen.

He was strong and brave.
A wet tongue licked his hand.
"Good boy, Stormy," he said.
"You're brave too."
He put his arm around the yellow dog,
his new friend.

Afterword

The hurricane and storm surge that destroyed Galveston on September 8, 1900, is the nation's worst natural disaster. No one knows for sure how many people died, but it is estimated between 7,000 and 8,000. The storm wiped away more than 20,000 houses and damaged thousands of buildings.

The Weather Bureau, a government agency that forecast weather, had a station in Galveston. The bureau predicted a severe storm, but not the furious hurricane or its deadly storm surge that flooded the entire island.

Once the storm began, weather instruments blew away. It is believed the winds raged between 130 and 140 miles per hour. Water flooded the low-lying city with waves higher than 15 feet. The waves pushed a ridge of rubble two stories high. This wall of debris wiped out everything in its path.

The huge brick and stone Ursuline Convent was surrounded by a high brick wall. When the wall broke, floodwaters poured into the building. The nuns leaned out windows and used poles to rescue people. A woman in a trunk floated by, and the nuns pulled her inside to safety. She was one of eight women who had babies in the convent that night.

After the storm, people rebuilt the city. They built a seawall and took other measures to protect Galveston from future storm surges. The wall was 7 miles long, 17 feet high, and 16 feet thick at its base. When another hurricane struck Galveston in 1915, the seawall prevented many deaths. In 1961, Hurricane Carla swept through coastal Texas. Again, the seawall protected Galveston from the heavy storm surge.

N

LOUISIANA

TEXAS

Galveston

GULF
OF
MEXICO

Bibliography

BOOKS

Coulter, John, ed. *The Complete Story of the Galveston Horror.* Chicago: J. H. Moore & Co., 1900.

Green, Nathan. *Story of the 1900 Galveston Hurricane.* Gretna, LA: Pelican Publishing Company, 1999.

Greene, Casey Edward, and Shelley Henley Kelly, eds. *Through a Night of Horrors: Voices from the 1900 Galveston Storm.* College Station: Texas A&M University Press, 2002.

Grubin, David. *"America 1900." American Experience.* WGBJ Educational Foundation: David Grubin Productions, 1998.

Larson, Erik. *Isaac's Storm: A Man, a Time, and the Deadliest Hurricane in History.* New York: Crown Publishers, 1999.

Lester, Paul. *The Great Galveston Disaster.* Gretna, LA: Pelican Publishing Company, 2000.

WEBSITES

CNN Specials—The Galveston Hurricane
   http://www.cnn.com/SPECIALS/2000/galveston

Galveston and Texas History Center at the Rosenberg Library
   http://www.gthcenter.org/exhibits/storms/1900/index.html

The Galveston Hurricane of 1900
   http://www.eyewitnesstohistory.com/galveston.htm

The 1900 Storm: Galveston, Texas
   http://www.1900storm.com

NOAA's Galveston 1900 Hurricane
   http://www.history.noaa.gov/stories_tales/cline2.html